Winnie
Dresses
Up

LAURA OWEN & KORKY PAUL

OXFORD

Helping your child to read

Before they start

* Talk about the back cover blurb. What might go wrong when Winnie enters a fancy dress race?
* Which of the two stories does your child think sounds the funniest, and why?

During reading

* Let your child read at their own pace – don't worry if it's slow. They could read silently, or read to you out loud.
* Help them to work out words they don't know by saying each sound out loud and then blending them to say the word, e.g. *c-ir-c-u-s, circus.*
* If your child still struggles with a word, just tell them the word and move on.
* Give them lots of praise for good reading!

After reading

* Look at page 48 for some fun activities.

Contents

OXFORD
UNIVERSITY PRESS

Great Clarendon Street, Oxford OX2 6DP

Oxford University Press is a department of the University of Oxford.
It furthers the University's objective of excellence in research, scholarship,
and education by publishing worldwide. Oxford is a registered trade mark
of Oxford University Press in the UK and in certain other countries

"Big Top Winnie" was first published in *Winnie Goes Batty* 2010
"Winnie's Fun Run" was first published in *Winnie on Patrol* 2010
This edition published 2018

British Library Cataloguing in Publication Data

Data available

ISBN: 978-0-19-276522-2

3 5 7 9 10 8 6 4

Printed in China

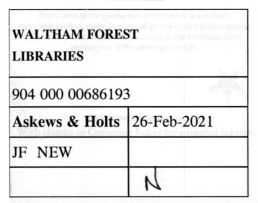

Big Top Winnie

✦ Chapter ✦ One

The circus had come to Winnie's village. Winnie and Wilbur went to see it. Winnie was very excited. She had never been to the circus before. Everyone was there.

"Look, look, Wilbur!" she said. "Hee hee, look at the clowns! They look as silly as a hippo in pigtails! Ha ha, that little dog is stealing the sausages!"

Then suddenly, Winnie went quiet.

"Ahhh!" said the crowd. A lady in a sparkly costume was walking along a rope, high up in the air.

The lady threw sparkly stars down onto the crowd.

"Oooh!" said Winnie.

The sparkly lady bowed, and everybody cheered. They whistled and they shouted and they clapped.

"Oooh, Wilbur," said Winnie. "I'd love it if people cheered like that for me!"

As Wilbur and Winnie walked home, Winnie tried walking like the sparkly lady.

First, she walked along the lines in the pavement, her arms spread out like the wings of an aeroplane.

Wibble-wobble, step-step.

"See?" said Winnie. "Look how good I am at this, Wilbur!"

Then Winnie tried walking along a garden wall.

Wibble-wobble, step-whoops!

She tried to balance herself by waving one leg and two arms around.

"I'll do it along the washing line!" she told Wilbur. "Just like that lady!"

But by the time they got home Winnie didn't just want to walk a tightrope. She had decided to put on a whole big circus of her own.

"There's no point without people to watch me. I'll do it for the little children at the school," she said. "They can cheer me and clap and say, 'Ahh! Isn't she beautiful!'"

"Meeow!" said Wilbur, who didn't think that was very likely.

★ Chapter ★ Two

When they got home, Winnie said,
"**Abracadabra!**" and suddenly, Wilbur was
wearing a pair of sparkly pants.

"You're my assistant, Wilbur," said Winnie. "Do a twirl!"

Twiddle-splat.

Wilbur wasn't much good at twirling.

"Woof-hee-hee!" laughed Scruff, the dog from next door, as he looked through the fence.

Wilbur growled. "Meeow."

"You can be my other assistant, Scruff!" said Winnie. "Just a moment . . . **Abracadabra!**"

And there was Scruff in a little sparkly waistcoat and a silly hat.

"Do a twirl, Scruff!" said Winnie.

Twiddle-splat.

Scruff growled. "Woof."

14

"Mee-hee-hee-ow!" laughed Wilbur.

Wilbur and Scruff chased each other
around the garden.

Leap!

Hiss!

Yap!

"Jerry!" Winnie called to her neighbour who was a giant. "Can you make me a tent, please?"

"OK, Winnie," said Jerry, and he set to work.

Crash! Bang! Rip! Stitch!

Jerry spent a little while looking for useful things in Winnie's cupboards and down the back of her armchair. When he couldn't find everything he needed, he went into the garden, and kept looking.

It wasn't long before he had made a strange kind of big top tent from a couple of trees, Winnie's curtains, and the lace from her best underwear.

"Abracadabra!"

The tent had jazzy bunting and colourful balloons.

16

"Right!" said Winnie. "Now the children can come and see my show. I'll just ring the teacher, Mrs Parmar."

Winnie waved her wand again.

"**Abracadabra!**" She made a stall selling candy moss and snotty apples.

Soon, the children arrived.

"Oooh!" they said when they saw the circus tent.

"Yuck!" they said when they saw the food. "When does the show start?"

"Er ... just a moment," said Winnie. **"Abracadabra!"**

Suddenly, Winnie was wearing the
sparkliest costume you've ever seen. It was
covered in glittery jewels. **Twinkle!**

"Can you play the music, please, Jerry?"
said Winnie.

"There isn't any music!" said Jerry.

"Boo!" went the children.

"DO something, Jerry!" said Winnie.

"Um ti-ti, rum ti-ti," sang Jerry.

Boom! Scruff played the drum.

Crash! Wilbur banged two saucepan lids together.

"Here I go!" said Winnie.

⭐ Chapter ⭐ Three

Winnie climbed up to the top of the ladder, then stepped carefully onto the rope.

Wibble-wobble-splat! Winnie fell head-first, onto her nose.

"Ha ha ha!" went the children. "More! More! More!"

"Ouch!" said Winnie. "Er ... I'll do some flying next."

Winnie flew around on her broom. Left. Then right. The children had seen her flying before.

"Boring!" shouted the children. "Boo!"

"Watch this, then!" said Winnie.

Wibble-wobble-wibble! She carefully stood up on the broom and stuck her arms out.

"Ta-daa!" went Jerry.

"Ah!" said the crowd.

"Do I look beautiful?" shouted Winnie.

"Meeeeooww!" went Wilbur. But it was too late.

Splat! Winnie flew into the rope and got all tangled up. She was hanging upside-down, high above the crowd.

"Help!" shouted Winnie.

"Hee! Hee! Ha! Ha!" laughed the
children. "Winnie's so funny!"

Jerry the giant lifted Winnie down, but
her shoes stayed tangled up in the rope.

"You can wear my shoes!" said Jerry, so
Winnie put them on. They were enormous.

"Ha! Ha!" went the children. "Winnie looks like a clown!"

When Winnie tried to walk, she tripped over Scruff. She landed in a bucket full of water.

"Ha! Ha! Haa!" went the children.

Winnie picked up another bucket of water. Winnie chased Scruff, Wilbur chased Winnie, and Jerry chased Wilbur.

"Hooray!" shouted the children, as they all tripped over each other. Bump-bump-bump-bump!

"They like us now that we're silly!" said Winnie. "Come on, Wilbur! Chase me!"

"Hee! Hee! Ha! Ha!" went the children.

At the end of the show, Mrs Parmar said, "That was very funny, Winnie!"

"We love you, Winnie!" said the children.

"Really truly?" said Winnie. She blew her nose on a hanky. **Snort!** "It can be more fun to be funny than to be beautiful," she said.

Winnie's Fun Run

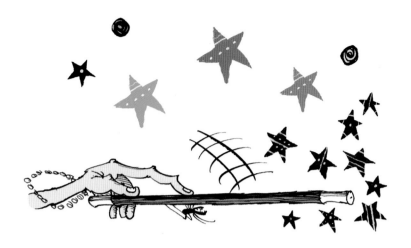

✦ Chapter ✦ One

Crash! Winnie opened the door.

"I'm home, Wilbur!" she shouted. "Where are you?"

Wilbur was having a nap just inside the door. He opened one eye, then closed it again.

"Wiiiiillllbuuurrrr!" yelled Winnie. "Guess what, Wilbur?"

Wilbur just looked at her.

"There's a fun run this afternoon!" said
Winnie. "Everyone has to wear fancy dress!
There are prizes for the best costumes! Oooh,
what costume shall I have, Wilbur?"

Wilbur rolled his eyes.

"**Abracadabra!**" went Winnie,
and suddenly she was dressed as
a mermaid.

But when Winnie tried to walk, she went
wobble-splat-crash! Mermaids can't walk
very well. They are even worse at running.

"Bother!" said Winnie. "I need to
be able to run in my costume. I know!
Abracadabra!"

At once, Winnie became a ballerina.
She twirled and swirled and twiddled and
twaddled until ...

Crash!

"Drat!" said Winnie, rubbing her leg.
"That's no good either!"

"Meeow!" said Wilbur. He had a good
idea. He pointed to a picture of a handsome
knight and a princess.

"What a great idea!" said Winnie.
"Clever cat, Wilbur!"

⭐ Chapter ⭐
Two

"**Abracadabra!**" Winnie was wearing a suit of armour. **Clang! Wobble-clash-crash!**

"Ouch!" said Winnie, rubbing her head. "Er … did you mean the princess, Wilbur?"

"Meeow!" said Wilbur.

"**Abracadabra!**" At once, Winnie was dressed as a princess. Her dress was frilly, and very, very colourful.

"Oooh, I like this one!" said Winnie.
"I'll be the prettiest runner of all, won't I,
Wilbur?"

"Meeow!" said Wilbur again.

"I'll win the prize for the best costume, easy-peasy, elephant-sneezy!" said Winnie. "I might even win the prize for the fastest runner, too. I wonder if I can run in this dress?"

Winnie took a step. Then she took another step. She did a little jig. Then she ran around the room.

"This is brilliant for running in!" she said. "Now I need an energy drink to keep me going."

Winnie found a bottle of pond water. She added some bat-pee squash.

"I need some food, too," said Winnie.
"Oooh, this will make me go fast!" She mixed
some tigers' toenails with rocket engine oil.
Then she held her nose and ate a big spoonful.

"Oooh, that is disgusting!" she said. "It's bound to make me go faster, though!" And Winnie was right. It made her go very fast . . . to the loo!

When Winnie came out of the loo, she didn't look well at all.

"I'm too weak and wobbly to race!" she cried.

Wilbur helped Winnie get to the fun run field. She tried running on the spot – but she just ran out of breath. "Oooh, Wilbur, it's no good!" she said. "I can't run!"

Then Winnie had an idea. "I'll make some trainers that can do the running for me! What a brilliant plan!"

"Meeow?" said Wilbur.

"**Abracadabra!**" went Winnie, pointing her wand at her princess shoes.

Zap! Her shoes turned into super-sporty speedy trainers.

"On your marks!" said the race leader. "Get set … GO!"

⭐ Chapter ⭐ Three

Winnie was way out in front.

Boing-boing! Leap!

"Wow!" shouted Winnie. "These trainers are amazing! Watch me go!"

But Winnie's new trainers were a bit naughty. They made Winnie run away from the race. They made her run through a hedge and through a haystack. Winnie couldn't stop running and she was covered in hay!

"Meeow!" said Wilbur. He had a good
idea to help Winnie stop. He spotted Jerry
the giant in the crowd. Wilbur got Jerry to
stand with his arms out.

Then Wilbur saw Jerry's dog, Scruff.
"Meeow, meeow!" said Wilbur to Scruff.

"Woof!" said Scruff. That meant he was
going to help too.

Meanwhile, Winnie was running through the market. She kept knocking things over.

Bang! Tumble! Squash! Splat!

"Help!" shouted Winnie.

Pant, pant!

But Winnie's trainers were running and running … back to the race field. And there was Jerry with his arms out.

Oomph!

Winnie ran slap bang into Jerry. Jerry lifted Winnie off the ground. Her trainers still wanted to run! But Scruff and Wilbur pulled them off Winnie's feet.

"Grrrr!"

"Hiss!"

Off ran the trainers, all on their own. They are probably running still.

At last, Winnie could stop.

"Oooh, I'm as shaky as a slug slime jelly. I never want to run again!" she said.

It was the end of the race – and time to find out who had won. "The winner of the best fancy dress costume is Winnie the Witch!" said the race leader.

"Hooray!" shouted the crowd.

"Oh!" Winnie was very pleased. "Come with me to fetch the prize, Wilbur!" she said.

Wilbur helped Winnie wobble up onto the stage.

"Here is your prize," said the race leader. "All the judges loved your scarecrow fancy dress costume."

"Scarecrow?" said Winnie. "But I'm not a . . ."

Wilbur put a paw over Winnie's mouth and dragged her off the stage.

"Ah, well," said Winnie. "I'd rather be a winning scarecrow than a princess, anyway."

"Meeow," agreed Wilbur.

After reading activities

Quick quiz

See how fast you can answer these questions!
Look back at the stories if you can't
remember.

1) In "Big Top Winnie", what does Jerry use
   to make Winnie's circus tent?
2) In "Big Top Winnie", what happens when
   Winnie puts on Jerry's shoes?
3) In "Winnie's Fun Run", how does
   Winnie stop running in the end?

1) a couple of trees, Winnie's curtains and the trimmings of her best
underwear. 2) she trips over things and makes the children laugh.
3) Jerry catches her.

Talk about it!

* If you could take part in a circus, what
  would you be? A tightrope-walker, an
  acrobat, a clown . . . or something else?

* In "Winnie's Fun Run", Winnie says
  "I'd rather be a winning scarecrow than
  a princess, anyway." Do you agree?